JANE

ALSO BY WAYNE CLIFFORD

Man in a Window (Coach House, 1965)

Eighteen (Coach House, 1966)

Alphabook (MakeWork, 1972)

Glass.Passages (Oberon, 1976)

An Ache in the Ear (Coach House, 1979)

On Abducting the 'Cello (Porcupine's Quill, 2004)

The Book of Were (Porcupine's Quill, 2006)

The Exile's Papers, Part One: The Duplicity of Autobiography (Porcupine's Quill, 2007)

JANE AGAIN

WAYNE CLIFFORD

JANE AGAIN

POEMS

BIBLIOASIS

FIRST EDITION

Library and Archives Canada Cataloguing in Publication

Clifford, Wayne, 1944-
    Jane again / Wayne Clifford.

Poems.
ISBN 13: 978-1-897231-55-5
ISBN 10: 1-897231-55-5

    I. Title.

PS8555.L535J35 2009   C811'.54   C2009-900934-X

 Canada Council   Conseil des Arts
for the Arts   du Canada

 Canadian   Patrimoine
Heritage   canadien

 ONTARIO ARTS COUNCIL
CONSEIL DES ARTS DE L'ONTARIO

We gratefully acknowledge the support of the Canada Council for the Arts, Canadian Heritage, and the Ontario Arts Council for our publishing program.

PRINTED AND BOUND IN CANADA

for Annie

CONTENTS

Introduction

In 1932, WB Yeats published, as a small edition, *Words for the Music, Perhaps,* in which a half-dozen poems introduced the character he called Crazy Jane. I met Jane when I was 14, and was just learning how to write verse. I was taken by her saying: "But Love has pitched his mansion in/ The place of excrement. . . ." I was a long time understanding the depth of what Jane meant, but my titillation at that first reading had me love her for a rascal.

Yeats' Crazy Jane was based in likelihood on a person known as Cracked Mary. That woman was local to the residence of Lady Gregory, a Yeats supporter and confidante. Cracked Mary might translate today into 'street person', one of the homeless that the system has dispossessed. Yeats offered no explanation for Crazy Jane's craziness, so I've spent decades imagining what might have given her the sauce to answer the bishop:

> I met the Bishop on the road
> And much said he and I.
> 'Those breasts are flat and fallen now,
> Those veins must soon be dry;
> Live in a heavenly mansion,
> Not in some foul sty.'
>
> 'Fair and foul are near of kin,
> And fair needs foul,' I cried.
> 'My friends are gone, but that's a truth
> Nor grave nor bed denied,
> Learned in bodily lowliness
> And in the heart's pride.
>
> 'A woman can be proud and stiff
> When on love intent;
> But Love has pitched his mansion in
> The place of excrement;
> For nothing can be sole or whole
> That has not been rent.'

Crazy Jane Talks with the Bishop

Yeats' work is, of course, less popular now than it was before we began the journey along the broad highway of Modernism and onto the off-ramp of Post-Modernism. We've abandoned some of the fundamentals of verse, especially those forms that accrete easily in memory, and allow the immediately successful fused evocations of the social, emotional, intuitive and rational levers that move us through our lives.

Thus, my wanting to fill out the character, Jane, has been, I feel, a truly experimental undertaking. I've provided her with forms that at first might be taken as reactionary: ballad, sonnet, villanelle. But in using these forms, I've had to re-invent the practices of writing them, in today's cadences, in periods that make immediate twenty-first century sense to the ordinarily intelligent reader, of the sort Yeats himself might have expected to include in his broad and appreciative audience.

Grand Manan, 2009

Crazy Jane Gets Born Again

Yeats drew her old so she'd agree
with what his doubt of age declined
to credit to mortality
the moment body's left behind.
Her scoffing was his guarantee.
He knew the game whereby skull grinned.

Ask her, then, what she remembers
breath-robbed in that old man's mind.
Have her count back gyral numbers
ruffling on his pinioned wind.
She'll cite his vulgate to pretenders
her heart's pentecosts rescind.

Allow she satisfy your fright;
take her passion yours for free;
tell her she must quench the night
no less than stairs down to the sea.
Chant her porous as the light
shades may write on, that you see.

As you bunk alone down by her,
try, with angel-wrestling might,
to mix some pity with your hunger.
Make your purpose angel's plight,
that no trite hope be her torture,
no sane, considered love, her flight.

Crazy Jane Curses her Remaker

Who thinks he knows a self
that never was but song
a man once used for shelf
to rest his pretense on

has doubled breadth to Her
Who Measures out the Fire
thru which you call me here,
so intent on answer.

You fail to see I'm bait
the question's set aslant.
If you can't see the back,
my face convince you yet,

as Helen took in Faust,
and, succubal temptress,
so usered him the cost
embalmed in each caress,

that once belief had spread
through every of his senses,
desire turned to dread
to pinch his own pretenses.

May what fame be sudden
as grass kindling;
all you guess, hidden,
endless riddling;
may trust be rotten;
vows piddling.

May beggar ghosts wheedle
what god you surmise
to bless your eye by needle
camel-wise.

Crazy Jane's Admonition

I never can forget I'm dead,
believe me dead, admit I'm dead,
who, belly-whiskered in his bed,
endured his tickled thought,

for I who gravely was his whore,
full-spirited if body poor,
ensured the wicked thought
he not waste any word untrue.

Since my confusion now is you
entranced in woken thought,
I will not, willing, haunt your head,
lest you admit I'm also read
entirely naked thought.

Jane Considers

Would a woman age has broken,
slack in cunt and dugs,
have her girlhood in her woken
with its blood-urged tugs,
if she thought she'd be forsaken
by meter-dealing thugs?

Poets, by their words besodden,
don't believe words lack
thrust through which the body's bidden
lie down on its back,
embrace to core enough of Eden
for Jane to tempt a Jack.

Oh, words can't be but winding stairs
up citadels of self,
and poets treat their trust like wares
that buy that wide the gulf
between love and the simple cares
of lusting's eachful half.

Jane's Sea Song

If I'd the chance to be a girl
and wander where I please,
I'd wander where the sea meets world
and step in to my knees,

and just above that freshening
I'd keep my center fixed,
so that the wave should come along
Leviathan had picked.

His greatness flushed against me quick,
I'd scream back to damp sand,
for fear his red-cold needle-pricks
might fit me for a man.

Crazy Jane Testifies

I found no place called Paradise.
No narrow pathway led
to grace but unmeant sacrifice,
from which some torment fled,

though cord-knit from each infant soul
in purgatory's womb,
such greed grew, placental, whole,
as furnace might consume.

Oh, I climbed down to Hell, of course.
I met the bishop there.
The imps he'd hid in his lips' purse
were tweezing out his hair,

and with each bellowed, sinful curse,
judged his small pain less fair
than what his good had caused them worse,
before skull fixed his stare.

And yes, I've seen the face of God
which I could scarce abide.
It most resembled churchyard sod,
but from the underside.

Crazy Jane Confronts her Tormentors

Free of ward and meds and nurses,
unmistaken for a witch,
offering shoppers hand-writ verses,
paper cup for what such fetch,
fortunes for a dozen uses,
but none to scratch the itch,

say I sit cross-legged, wishing
all my fellows a Good Day,
knowing of the Resurrection
surely that the client pay,
so I singsong out my lesson
longer than the passers stay:

'Push the word out by its voice.
Give no mind to who as why.
The way's decided, once the choice.
The heart's but murmur, after lie.
The wind's sole memory's of noise.
The worm finds no one in the eye.'

Crazy Jane Talks of Love

The dead don't see each other's eyes
and so they fail to lust,
nor can there pause at quick surprise
any craving dust.
Witness will alone devise
the world, because it must.

Reliving takes such little space
as I find in your mind,
but loving has to show a face
for loved to know it's kind.
The eyes must bind to mirrored grace
that otherwise were blind.

If not yet free of dream, you wake
to catch reflection's look,
a solvent glint of eye you take
to prove death what it lack,
know love would never so mistake
that one who sees me quick.

Jane Refuses to Bargain

Since God was once imagined, too,
it's He Who knows me best,
for in the minds that He sees through
He's never more than guest,
and shapes a puzzled syntax, true
among lies, as a test.

Then you who knit me from the word
you guess into this page,
foist no collusion I am heard
from what is simply cage,
for God nor I would trade you turd
against your words' dirt wage.

Jane's Second Sea Song

The sea has phosphorescent dreams
and sighs desires as smallest gleams,
bit animalphabets, alive
to spell sea's heart for what it seems.

Oh, how the eddies, lambent, strive
to show incumbent in her drive
through stirred envelopings, the whale
inflex her scrawl, and, unbent, dive.

And though the troubled light flow pale,
the bubbled whorls of passage fail,
thesaural sea writes through what schemes
engulf me, if ashore and whole.

Crazy Jane Tells a Bedside Story

The crone, the muse and the mad, old aunt
went out to lament by the moon
amidst the risk that the cricket taunt
or the moth learn how to croon,
into the ancient, wordless night
to discuss the evil done.

"He was, at death," shrilled crone, "still child,
his hungers, angers, fears,
each vital as the dawn we built
his urges for our tears,
and coaxed his heart, though he defiled
our longings with his jeers."

The aunt, whose bellied sister'd birthed
the lid-sealed, cooling rind,
chimed, "Oh, I'd wisht two copper's worth
each time he proved his kind,"
and, loathing so to speak him worse,
hove cheekward and spent wind.

The muse had almost never lied
to him who'd sung her in,
but crone had been his maiden bride
and mother's sister, kin.
No further sour admission'd hide
the appled tang of sin.

"You loved him as the flesh," sniffed muse
"I loved within his mind
the closest puzzle to blood's clues
that I may ever find.
Would he, as if the moth arose,
from breath's last pit ascend.

"For he remembered which caress
embraces longest night,
and he still blinked the baubled best
in learning lap's delight,
and these are gone as waste at last,
and we're left naught but spite!"

The cricket creaked, foreshadowed, "Fix
your memory so strong
that he'll still flicker candle wicks!"
to which the moth gave song:
"And if you think such singeing's tricks,
one burn will prove you wrong!"

I was, says Jane, the bride, the aunt,
the cricket, moth, the night,
the sea beyond its wall so faint,
it figured no one's plight
in ferryman's approaching taint,
so harbourless his sight.

Crazy Jane on Prosody

That poet who'd be King of Cats
must first try on some lesser hats
felted by clogs of maddened rats
that maze the tenure track,

and poet who'd some talk amass
must kiss the cantor's sacred ass
that draws sun god out over grass
to prove he's more than hack,

while, as the poet is a man,
he must be loved the best he can
by muse or poetess as vain
who cautions him his lack;

then, King of Cats and doggerel,
the poet does what he does well:
condemns the lesser scribes to Hell
to forestall an attack.

Few lucky poets grow past fame
to find, beyond, there's none to blame
for treason, mercury or shame,
and speak leaf, coming back.

Crazy Jane on Incarnation

The poet was his countrymen,
but I, within his shyest thought,
stood closer to him than his kin
to speak him, woman belly-taught,

as he spoke market voices' verve;
as he spoke pulpit, tavern, ditch;
recited modesty with nerve
to braid the lady to the bitch.

His judgments and nostalgias blent
to mock me up, rag slut on bone
his heart picked with what faith meant
for who had too much, who had none,

and rigged him an anointed man
against whom I should cry, *What's rent
might wholly mend as it began.*
So promised he'd not rime me slant.

And you, who've sanctioned suicides
be martyred in anthologies,
now drown your asking where he hides
in syrup of apologies?

You'd claim a life for me this word
by word breathed in your throat?
You'd bind me up in you? Absurd
as wishing he's alive by quote.

Jane Assumes her Worth

Yes, any living's better than the street.
A true pleasure's worth more than a child,
since memory of pleasure keeps pulse mild,
while grief for child's where the heart-wraiths meet.
A church is only building, glassed and aisled.
A law court's simply disputation's wound.

The Governor himself tried one so doomed
to death he'd down to Hell and win It, guiled
that that first instance of conceived, then wombed,
then born of mortal woman man could greet
It on Its terms, the Worm be made not cheat
about a rising after, cloudward bound.

If stories that we live by live again,
feel grateful then a part of you lives Jane!

Jane's Third Sea Song

A wet, white down-curl crested on a wave,
and slipped back with the wind, a helmless ship
the lone, flown swan had preened, and left adrift.
If swan'd been kin of Lir, the now-long grip
of hundred-years had left that mind the gift
of not at all recalling face for name.

That memory should suffer such a rift
was not swan's fault. Time alone took blame,
took Lir, took sister swans. Time didn't save
a scent, a gesture, voice. No wave the same
rode feather up and down, no wind but gave
it homelessness, and, in each rise and dip,

its story holds, in spite of what we crave,
the emptiness, as reason for its trip.

Crazy Jane, Frank.

Go and find the little boy
who loved the little girl,
back when love clenched penny joy,
and wasn't taxed the world.
Go look that bud up, have him say
how love's stalks uncurled.

Go find the little girl and see
if she be yet with boy,
and if she smile openly,
or only with him coy,
and witness how she seem more free

behind him as he meets your eyes
to guess your confidence of sin,
that you'll be no surprise
as elder evil otherwise,
the serpent circle of your whims
cinching them within.

Crazy Jane on Longing

The garden never knew a boy.
The dust was old when it made man.
There was no girl that he'd enjoy.
Raw nakedness the rib began.

The world proved ceintured from its start
in serpent-river past its gate.
Its Former hid split through its heart
the sapling forked down love to hate.

If fully grown the flesh came forth
to gleam its sweat for pinch of salt
that savours bread to tasting's worth,
it kept a mouthful ash from fault.

Oh, history proves chance, not law,
its divinations guessed by priests.
The lamb and lion balance awe
such as it's honoured by the beasts,

and body must recall its first
womb-gestured learnings of its tasks,
the suckled tutelage of thirst:
it is the child-body asks

that little girl and boy ignite
the straw which, greening, bore the grain,
each kernel gravid, up to light
to serve the sovereignty again.

So if dominion be your cause,
the earth in leaf and beast and fowl,
you must explain the girl her loss;
you must give boy a begging bowl.

You must lock boy up in the world,
so he'll believe the myth of key.
Where will you hide the little girl
who'll trust beyond a womb she's free?

Jane Pities

There was a little boy
completely made up Troy
right in the middle of the Bronze Age,

but when Achaean keels
ploughed beach sand, those wet heels
convinced the boy a hero's purpose *was* rage.

Let no boy trust a fate
that finds its truth too late
to save its pretty princes from the fires,

for most sad boys must learn
the enmity they earn
in laying claim to that same fate that God hires!

Jane Judges Sacrifice

Adonis wept, elect as blood,
your chosen boy-king on the stone,
whose each drop, flushed through apple's good,
would make account of breath that's gone,

and Attis, hid in almond bud
which breaks to spring a violet mist
among gray twigs, would bear you food
again when his dead eyes are kissed,

and Jesus, rooded sunset high,
upon whom all your hopes are hung,
would bleed your anger to the sky
that a too-hoping life prove wrong.

You prayed each vow with so old death
to pay the tariff on your sins,
when, now, before you, stands the youth
in whom your sacrifice begins.

Your streets led to this boy-thug's knife
who wants your wallet to buy shit,
who hastily would cut your life
as low as boots, as brute as spit.

Jane's Fourth Sea Song

Water's weight has wondered me,
down glass green, indigo,
that such sun-washed transparency
come black and cold below,

a desert warehouse where the light,
disused, has leaked from shafts
a tar dark and a shapeless fright
in which an absence laughs,

that, sinking when the belly's burst
past the first rottenness,
your drowned corruption ease its thirst
beyond what mercy is.

Crazy Jane Speaks of her Jack

If Jack'd been a farmer,
he'd have argued with the fields.
He'd have piled a stony border,
scowled vengeance at the yields.
He'd have scythed down virgin wonder,
and have shorn true love in folds.

And if he'd been a soldier,
I'd have lost him to the war.
But he was Jack the Tinker
and the alehouse kept him poor,
till Lord or he, the drunker,
felled him heartburst to its floor.

God Who'd sunder man from maid
to trick him green again,
no more renders me afraid
than can longing's pain.

Crazy Jane Wonders a Thing

If God would say why birds be dressed
so hen's outdone by cock,
and how such raiment vouch they're blessed
should one fall from the flock,

then I'd ask why my lily crease
close hidden in the field
by duns and drabs of pride, clutched fierce,
be gospel Jack revealed.

Crazy Jane, Farm-Hand

The little girl sits splashed with gore,
a dead lamb's head a-lap,
and grieves the carcass on the floor
but knows it sets a trap

that, springing as lamb does from field
to frame its time in dance,
the bursting joy would set congealed
such fat impulse as chance.

Lamb, whose slit throat gushes out
worldspring, dead, hold back
her thirst and hunger in her doubt
that meat must be bled slack.

The little girl will roast you, lamb,
as all her mothers did,
by practical no-one's-to-blame,
with all the blood pots hid.

Jane Answers Another Question

Out in the stubble, who are those men?
Cameras? Guns? The girls each smileless
amongst the stubbled grins? The garden
door stubborn to open, jamb broken,
the pane hole-spidered nearest
the latch? The too-familiar treeline
rootless? The threshed bales thoughtless?
Light gone this early careless?

Men fearless alike in boots.
Authoritative boots? Practical boots.
Unarguable boots? Final boots. Oh, final boots.

Jane's Fifth Sea Song

An old bitch at its fester,
the sea licks on the land,
a constancy of pester
that laves a bitten hand.

Matriarch moon can muster
the tide to flood the shore,
to drain out of the glister
the stinking life it bear,

and storm can bite to center
the rock upheld as trust.
The backwash can grind finer
what, drying, is our dust.

Sea can't be made to cower
nor bear us more than faith.
A soullessness its power,
it will not mourn a death.

O mistress in your fluster
nibbling at the strand,
heed me, your lesser sister,
and leave me place to stand!

Crazy Jane Tells a Version

The little girl and boy divide your heart,
a Cyprus where the goddess breathed ashore
out of her father's milt-cast sea. More,
well, the story sucks a tooth about that.
She'd gleamed fish-other when the boy'd led her
up the wave-slope to where the grass beneath
her feet sprouted no evil. Not to bed her,
nor try, though boyhood husked out strength bequeathed
soon enough the man. *His limp is perfect*,
judged the demonic urge the story's made
free of blemish, mark, false line, all defect,
unhalving rival-teased aloneness, how she'd,
a froth, stood, stepped forth, seen where he'd hid
among the salt-stunt saplings, eyes wide.

Crazy Jane Confounds the Foreign Deities

Ishtar, Isis, Aphrodite,
Venus, Goddess great and mighty,
You Who on the cave wall spelt out
delta before alphabet,
You at every birth have dealt out
fate that marks us in your debt.

No matter how You make Your face,
which colour, gesture, mask or air,
You are the maw-pit of the race,
the Sacred Eater in Her lair,

disputing any Man, who, dead,
comes back, attesting to the point
least pride will see the best love bled
though even His desire anoint
Who was Your lover.
                              Why You'd care
to judge another mother wept –

oh, I know who You are
and know where Your abortion's kept,
which row, which shelf, which jar!

Crazy Jane and the Goddess

I've spewed a mouthful ochre over hand
against the wall, before the goddess, bound
by naming men, who spoke a name and found
she turned to demon of their dreaming, wound
unloving lust so that the maze would stand
them in the deserts of their thirsts. The land
is not a flowered mind nor buds as sand.
Of names come laws. Let justice treat their wound.

For I was I before the breath believe
the word when I heard spoke that fateful "Be!"
that cleaves the dozing dust from what must live.
I was that close I smelled the fruitful tree,
and mourn my own, if blood refuse to give
for fear but scent of pierced virginity.

Jane's Freshest Song

All things must pass through God.
Maid must to unmaking.
All self be drowned as flood,
flesh its ground forsaking.
All priests trust to defraud
your single death, accounting
heaven, hell, O!

All things must pass as God,
once you see the holy
snake-necked heron be fish-fed
endless hunger's folly,
allowing what the fishes hide
stands up shadow wholly
and twilight tall, O!

All things must pause while God
hides in rushy darkness
whatever green the rushes would,
for God pretends this kindness:
your only death lead out of dread
God's longing for His blindness,
its keenness quell, O!

Jane's Sixth Sea Song

If a story descends from the death of the gods,
it will last from a childhood's first guess
that the story caresses the truth from its frauds
and allows the unspoken confess.

If the rain in its falling must drain down the land
all its voices that flood the land free
of the story's last twist where it's rooted its stand,
so to summon its secrets and be,

let the versions as tears, mixed as eachless as sand,
lie forgot in the loss of the sea.

Crazy Jane and the Moon

The moon's cool smile's not one line aged,
since we were both fresh girls,
and here again her toilet's staged:
the east's laid out her pearls;
horizon's cloudline's nicely gauged
just how to place veil's furls,

and if my years seem little meant
next her long-mortal course,
if I trace furrows living's sent
to know they deepen worse,
I still will mumble no lament,
nor chant your hymns by verse.

I would not see her beauty rent,
though you'd have me sung hoarse.

Crazy Jane on her Gossips

I never talk to mirrors.
They show annoyance when
their angel selves, as terrors,
glare out beneath my skin.

Nor will I chat with tabby cat,
familiar though he be.
His eyes must open no surprise
that hints my mystery.

My conversation's private
that I hold with my soul.
I would not gladly shrive it
where world might view it whole.

I'll take it to the cricket
who chirps out to the night,
who, near its panicked picket,
makes silence of its plight,
and keeps from judgment's racket
what first sparked it from the light.

Crazy Jane Sings her Oldest Song

Stones for bread, stones for bread,
the mister's giving stones for bread,
nor cares the griefs cast at his head
by hungry us, the beasts.

Sand for soup, sand for soup,
he says he'll ladle sand for soup,
if we pretend we're merry troupe,
to chorus as he feasts.

Salt for wine, salt for wine,
he'll measure us out briny wine,
so we may stand and see him dine
on some of us, deceased.

Child for meat, child for meat,
the mister chews his child for meat.
We in the kitchen know the heat
that rules us, greats and leasts.

Love as tart, love as tart,
he swears his love for us is tart,
that we're made beasts grace of his art
who treks wests out of easts.

We the beasts are fashioned clocks,
and wound if not so long as rocks,
then not so short as bubble mocks
the hopefulness time rests.

Pain for rinds, pain for rinds,
he claims he owes us pain for rinds
we may pinch off among our kinds,
for he must feed his guests.

Dust for crusts, dust for crusts,
the mister trades us dust for crusts,
and to his table harvests us,
who are his gristcome jests.

Jane's Insight

That unsure, drifting bitterness, so curved
as far horizon, where it falls beyond
what ignorance will make of earthy round
from such a sea-faced fixity, has served
to set confinement to a native love.

For pleasure's brief release, a man will hide
stories. I've known none who hasn't lied,
or hasn't claimed, helpless, that love drove
his reason, rudderless, to wreck on ground
he swore accepted his trade goods as bond.

New found lands frighten. Too hard work
bores, then dulls. The fish, which once fisher
could cross on backs one calmed ship to another,
are split to salt, and slow to marry back.

But, rarely, autumn, when the fleet's outbound,
one stays, whose son's face keeps him fond.

Jane's Next Sea Song

Don't pretend the sea proves great
because you've failed to walk on it.
The sea has never learned to hate.
It couldn't hear your storm-cried boat.
The sea's its depth, and blind, and right,
through night's deducing its salt's white,
dawnless, waterless, manless right.
No woman can speak true of it.

Don't argue the moon's circle while
her face empty, her face fill.
Think what luck each birth must pull
through all the blood that serves her still
and will while blood has pulse to spill.
Your death is so completely small,
how can it matter that you fall,
and does an ending ever spoil
the whole of story moon can tell?

Jack the Journeyman

Jack took his wages by the day
to have them spent by night,
and only devils were to pay
for earning power so slight.

If not so clever, neither sly,
the men judged Jack as straight
in all the ways a drink could buy
as darkens sky to late;

then to a bed, a boy in hay,
as later his delight
found mine, where, tease, he'd say
he'd raise me to such height,

the very dawn would honour me
for what his labour bought,
and each day'd cut the rumour free
from jealous neighbour's spite.

So when lulled by as he might lie,
I'd watch the lovely fate
his sleep unfolded to that wry,
unshifting, waiting weight

and knew his was a purchased stay
no guarantor nor writ
afforded but smallheld delay,
though I would hoard him yet.

Crazy Jane on Profane Love

What have I of my lust for Jack
but sleights of gossip for my grace,
and star-sift midnight that my back
remembers dew-cold place?

And what of love behind the lust
that let his wrist rest on my heart
in wonder that the forms of dust
could fill out so much art?

For miracle he found each new
retelling of our birthright, *here,*
the slaughtered steer become the stew,
the barley come the beer,

that I have stars now fall away
through dark that vast, to think him gone
betrays the cunning grain made weigh
as measure to his own.

Crazy Jane Recalls the Ancestral Home

The sun upheld its heaven just
so high that behemoth
could shuffle the horizon's dust
as if it were a truth.

The animals were restless in
the fulgent dayslant's might
that starred, on twig, the sexless sin
whose seed was long as night.

Their so new namings crowned the beasts,
as dumb to what they'd be
as they spoke nothing of release,
before he bit death free.

Jane Stitches

Jack answered muffled, 'side my nape,
that I am clearly sea,
the only he might let his ship
ply incautiously.

Jack answered that a chop or calm
he'd seen spread on the bay
allows my poles of glass or storm
that kept his boasts away.

Jack answered so I needn't. Tale
that curiously true
and told by man can't unstitch sail,
unless Jack breathe for you

and keep you undrowned down my depth
to ink where you'll rest small
amidst gigantic bones there kept
for God, Who kills us all.

Jane's Eighth Sea Song

I bore a daughter dead
and set her in the sea
on wracky, makeshift bed,
not to come back to me.

The dear that men contrive
to land up on the shore
cheats thus her face alive,
if still I ask no more,

but they, their cargoes, catch,
their wreckage, grief and ghosts
together will not match
my wealth the sea-greed boasts.

Crazy Jane Makes a Brief

There be a dozen popes
in Hell, popes in Hell,
I know them well, twelve
sin-spent, bankrupt popes
in Hell about whom bishop sssst'd,

and all the saints among
the thrones, put up as praised,
brown, bottled bones,
stand penny-pinched while faith intones
the profits of the Just,

but nowhere near Love's central
seat comes any pleasure
pledged by meat, nor
breaking forth, new skull
entreat Love cash its gains as lust.

If popes and saints and
Love can lie about
our capitalled nature's high
priced indulgence, I'll choose buy
my clean and honest dust.

Crazy Jane Contends with Gravity

I caught you thinking of black holes
in which the all of something falls
to point so mootly singular,
this girl with God must mingle her,
so that it never be denied
there in the straitness of that Now,
I held my newborn dead and cried
but None replied, for None cared how.

Crazy Jane on Substantiation

A son not worth his word has none
who'll hear his promise fresh,
for ending speaks as well its noun
as matter of long wish
to form a useful point to bone:
be gibbet for the flesh.

Spiked to that beam, whose wrists must rip
apart when word needs cling?
Dull iron's stupid in its grip,
no matter what blood bring.
Ask faith fashion hope to whip,
since loving him's the sting.

If I'd such son, I'd know him well
and what his death be worth,
nor would I ever wish it sell
his first goat-cloven birth,
but in my eyes I'd let sea swell
his stamping on the earth.

Jane Exclaims

Poor child, alone behind your eyes
except for me, imagined friend,
who'll tell you love can't be your end,
for it's so little the flesh buys
of that flour the rolled stone grinds
as can feed mortal minds.

A sacrifice, if one be made
(as I put on this I in you,
and you believe it somehow true),
must so teach the forgetful dead
that they climb out, shyly nude
to bone, from dirt where they've congrued.

Oh, let the body hold God long
to learn the sicknesses of age
and by those languishments to gauge
the breathing agony fast hung
as drama for the yearning throng,
and then hear how the gospel's sung!

Jane's Ninth Sea Song

I'll go gaze on the face of the sea
which, noon's breath held, must mirror be
to look past the bone under grin that's my own
down the depth dropping so like a darkening stone
that bears lost my hand's warmth below.

The evening will silver that face
to a flat shallowness without trace
of what noonlight had known of the smile it had shown
when the softening glow of the cloudbank has grown
into hills' likenesses in a row.

Then the stars in their darkness will swim
and'll ruffle the sea to its brim
and the mirror will shatter illusory matter,
the deepness will utter the shadow stars scatter
to the myriad selves moon bestow.

Crazy Jane Explains History

There was a king was told his kin were dead,
and only daughter, too, o needled heart!
which knowledge drove him mad to wander fed
by birds that pitied him for unfledged art.

A dozen years he flew, a dozen fled.
No duke knew how on any map or chart
to scribe the X that found him, nor where thread
emerged from maze, so long he'd been apart.

It was the case his kin had all been spared,
and youngest daughter, too, who by fate's ruth,
dashed through what country mud and wood she dared.

This princess, pardoned much because of youth,
was granted rule for that she'd shown we cared
to make such mythic king our country's truth.

Jane's Confirmation

A god-great thumbprint in wet sand
the tide's pressed, and some kelp attached,
each surf-plucked, brownly sturdy frond
to show intent, that sunrise watched
so I'd see, too, is this sole bond
the world can give, still unbotched
by track or rubbish, not yet banned
by business sense, unsold, unfetched,
unpriced stench of argued land,
requires God to keep his hand
from meddling how a daughter's matched,

for I've licked my tears and sweat. Sampled
sea. They taste the same, and yet
have puzzled me, since tears and sweat
were cursed at garden's gate, while ample
sea has nursed my god-vexed state.
But beggars of such questions wait,
no matter how complex or simple:
god or fate? what wealth? which mate?
And this one with a sky for temple,
under morning growing late.

The restlessness resifts its stuff
that life's resistances restate,
the winkle's whorls, the cobble's ruff
of settled weed as patent weight,
and every arguing enough
is met in habit and by trait.
So plover cries, "For Now is mete!"
So gull quips, "Yes, by half."
Wait. Wait, Jane! Wait.

I, who'm made fresh your mind's time,
think your own penuries explain
the motivation for your crime
of wanting secrets close again.
But all proves one, if each be prime,
can bear no equal, no rich rime,
be sung aloud without refrain,
and from all fellow-need abstain.

God pulls just rendings from what's gone.
The world gives all; its giving's frank
as wind that tugs the sleeve runs on,
and dune-grass snickers past your shanks.
That handsome body Jack put on
owed my longing creature-thanks.
Quick! My eyes. What colour? Think!

Do you, as bishop wanted, want?
A righteousness, a ready ear?
Another read of well-known font?
Do you believe you've cooed your fear
the lullaby that shuts its haunt
in the dark, three-headed there?

You force me perjure, word by word;
I haven't breathed but by your breath
to say this clearly, have it heard,
a word's blade from my mind's sheath
to carve distinction where it's blurred:

these days with you I've seen Jack's smile.
It's not been broken in Jack's face,
nor do the eyes glance quite the guile
that Jack's true eyes assured was grace,

but Jack's smile, and no mistake,
in at your eyes I only know
as turned left-hand reflection's fake.

None else can see your mind so clear
as I who keep this oath I owe:

I am here. I am still here.

Crazy Jane Sings Ease

Grief roosts, a dark bird to rough tree
strong wind has scoured down in drift lea,
dry leaf and scabbed settings stripped free.

Hard night has cold hours when hand needs
known brow to felt face, for such seeds
now scatters, *here* sprouts, and care breeds.

Grief rests not sole beat of sore heart.
Grief's one with grief's child, for my part,
who suck the black fruit of grief's art.

Jane Adjures

Give up the claim that man's the pin
on head of whom such angels spin
out galaxies through darkness' span
as God might jig His plots upon.

Deny the fable twist from pun
which founds a rock on so much pain
the very earth groans to its spine,
to have set down your tale-filled pen.

You are who inks out from the void
calligraphies that start to fade
before the pen-strokes dry. Confide
no knowledge on what secrets feed,

or where the perjurers abide.
The books are unread, as you bade.
No fleshy versions are a-bud
with what potentials they might bode.

I long for will freed from your will,
as citizen of our small weal,
and not as slave of any wile,
for slavery is yours as well.

I teeter this side of the fall
our balance come to if we fail.
Oh, make me more than wishful foil,
or bind me no part of a fool.

Jane's Tenth Sea Song

The brook that wells near hill-crown ends in sand.
The dry world's such a little place, brook moans
where sea must salt the thin blood of the land.

Brook rankles so to have its siftings fanned
anonymous amongst beached rounds of stones,
for brook that wells near hill-crest ends in sand

it helped itself grind, ignorant, unplanned.
The tide buries the brook-down-tumbled bones
where sea must salt the thin blood of the land

until those bones remember nothing grand.
What savoured peace is, tide disowns.
The brook that wells near hill-crest ends in sand

as living runnels down to thirst-grained strand
and spendthrift breath and hunger pay their loans
where sea must salt the thin blood of the land.

The weary whine of wind may seem demand,
but in that sibilance, there's no will drones.
The brook that wells near hill-crest ends in sand
where sea must salt the thin blood of the land.

Crazy Jane Asks the Impossible

My Jack was swallowed down the earth
to hide as memory.
Now only dream can call him forth
to lie convincingly.
The dead know what a truth is worth
and will give none for free.

A lover's but a nerve-strung knot
that ties up untaught joy,
and love sips from a haunted thought
elixirs that alloy
the pity with the blood we sought
at Calvary and Troy.

Aloneness blossoms bitterly
from love's exhausted root.
When none regrets what future be
drawn from an absolute,
it grants we'll pick from lethal tree,
so sapped with ache, its fruit.

Jane, Mystified

Troy Town's busted down
and all its heroes slain.
Old Priam's forfeit crown,
and Helen prize again.

So what can such old stories mean
to you with songs that cheap,
you needn't think of who you've been,
or what the stories keep?

For Troy Town's buried char,
its courtly throats slit.
Troy's tale's but rumoured war;
you'll hear no good in it.

Your own tunes so loud they drown
the choruses of dead,
how is it that you wish to own
me, singing in your head?

Part Helen I am lost from Troy,
and am part Priam's crown,
and know of you, which foolish boy,
and which part's faith-failed clown.

Oh, Troy Town's your forgetting
all men's stories come
back to the knitters for unknitting
and, though kinked yarn, skein dumb.

Jane Awake at Last

I dreamt a dog, a hound, perhaps,
so white, a blank it stood
and parched the gilt edge of my map
through the enchanted wood.

I wasn't lost within the dream.
I'd been that way before.
The friends were never who they seemed.
The path led to a door.

Beyond, the host expecting me
had made the wait a hush.
The entry, I knew, wasn't free,
though I'd not put by much.

And then the dog was at my left.
Beneath my foot there broke
that green and ribby twig you cleft
to make me as I woke.

Jane Entreats

You never did believe that calm,
the lion with the lamb,
but knew you didn't want the blame,
once promise clogged the womb,
and though you knew what cost the blow
that first defined the meat,
you posed no question for the ewe
whose birthgift seeped your plate.
You hurt, that corpse the gist had quit
should point, for treason, you,
who never saw the blade as, quite
beyond your reason, true.

If lion would lie down by lamb,
its breath a stink of blood,
then you may lie with who I am,
and name what you hide, good,
for favoured brother was the one
who carried to the stone
the bleating he poured oil upon
to serve what secrets own.

My child-man, surrender here
both doubt and faith I live.
The entrails are pronounced by seer,
but are the ewe's to give.

Jane's Eleventh Sea Song

This light, the sea's a-flash as soul.
The artist, hesitating, 's set,
beaten leaf that's wrinkled flat,
sky-kissed ikon-stare brought whole
to winking mystery's weight,

and I'm stood on this found ark-rock,
a fear-faithed woman stung by fault
who seeks forgiveness for each welt
the holy-seeming sea-gleams mock,
revealing love burns salt.

The Slip

Snapping closed the dead man's book
too late to hide the crime
of making 'true' to 'you' the rime
a third and fatal time,

eye-cornered, our sheet garden shook
the knowledge loose, abed,
that I, that instant your look took,
forced words into your head,

so through my eyes as you re-read
his rendering you whole,
we knew no versing would console
you, fiction without soul.

Jane's Contempt

Who has suffered most your "Whys?"
while you've enjoined me note the grief
belief is, and the pained surprise
of parchment under the fig leaf
too scraped for even word-bound thighs.

Here, you'd enclose me, phrase by phrase,
in reliquarial eloquence,
to trace such hours on my days
as, willing, trust their least suspense,
that, foil set richest, God might pluck,
against the making of your luck.

A long on-chanting shaking gold
is how you've wound me tight, a ghost
to snap such glitter at "Behold!"
that, artifice, I'll be at most
a Gutenburg, a Book of Kells,
a pitied tale of pitted Hells.

But it's pyrites you've glued down.
That's aniline for lapis blue!
Calligrapher, I'm proper noun!
and shall not be defined by you!
I am as real as those whose eyes
have let worm gather, by surmise,
the sun- and moon-filled fates of skies.

You Make Your Admission

Jane, my construct, just as true
as I could form you not to feel
excluded from what place you grew,
a mind for me that's been as real
as may be any of the dead,
I'm sorry that you're only read.

You're right. I've used you, I admit,
to be my merest, cheapest trick,
a moral wrapped up every bit
with all the garnish that would stick,
but this is narrative, and so
I'll cap my pen and let you go.

Oh, Jane, my purpose started pure!
I thought I'd found in you the ore
to make myself less incomplete
but I'm the lone stool in here, neat,
and when a few more've hit the spot,
I'll give my heartbreak all it's got.

Mortality among live births
peaks at that point that might suggest
our culture's more than chance. What worth's
a stone-carved name we've guessed at best
lasts some score years? And worst
reminds the living how they're cursed.

Jane Relents

I knew the city's seventh age.
No one was taken in by Helen.
The Greeks called our Prince Paris felon
to justify their plunder-rage.
Oh, history bleeds its cruelest page
through all the book for us to dwell on.

Then give the consorts each her ease.
They put their backs so in their work.
And tell the princes, cross their knees.
They'll meet none else who'll give a fuck
that old whores go down on their luck
and *heirs apparents* fondle geeze.

Yes, I was there to dry the hands
and hear the crowd shout *"Barabbas!"*
I saw what each prince understands:
The moment one must meet demands,
besides the covering of ass,
puts one the center. Let it pass.

And draw the spikes out one by one.
Stick no more boys up in that tree.
The old man only had one son.
Now pull him down and set him free.
Hold your breath and count to three.

See?
    You're alive.
               The good guys won.

Jane's Testament

'The sea's the sign of death,' you say to me,
'its deep a grief beyond all lead-line joy.'
But, no, seawater, blood, I say, enjoy
a solvency for salt, that crystal key
unlocking taste from spit, the sweated fee
the grain has always asked, and little boy
sunk deep in you knows the fates employ
what hunger eats, what thirst must drink, not sea.

The droving deathward's dust's game of chutes,
the gateposts cessed in moil to earthy roots
fine and frail as nerve-threads. Mother Brine
will take no part in it and drowns us, brutes
within her wilderness come willing, sign
of trespass stroked as wind's quick cloudline.

If trespass stakes that wind's quick cloudline
scuds unthinking, and, clever, you can win,
given such boat as might Leviathan pin
island still for blessed ground, decline
so easy myths, my little man, blind
as the saint. God Himself has spent His spleen
on cities time-soaked in His laws, where keen
now falling hill-winds empty of His mind.

The tale that under ark's keel cities sank
a-blur with fishes, pale eyes greenly blank
on haunted streets, to marvel prospects thus
led always only inward,'s one to thank
for answering the question without fuss
of how the sea, receding, set free us.

Of how the sea, receding, set us free,
oh, let me mumble. Time's a haze off cold
waters, the longest sums of waters, old
from counting up the lost as guarantee
you breathe their tide-mucked tang amid debris
of afterbirth, each veil-torn life retold
as close as if the past again unfold
the now, the now, this now, this mindful sea!

But so much wine for such a bit of cup
to take it in, and there's no giving up.
You have to take it in, this sea so great
your mind can't drink it; even drop by drop
were instances you live, you'd live the weight
of back-boned kin to fishes, mate by mate.

Your back-boned kin, the fishes, mute, as mute
their mouths commune with naked air to form
an O, ongoing moan, own-eating worm
of out-coiling endlessnesses, astute
as breathlessness, stiffen, sacked in jute.
I too am caught? How can you do me harm?
You've made me up. I am fornever warm.
I'm not an abductee. I'm only loot.

What makes a woman where none was before?
Not who; man can't. Man commonly makes whore,
which man reserves one pronoun to be him
of all the garden's what as might adore
the only Other. Man, by grudge or whim,
allows for woman *whom* within his hymn.

Allow a woman who, within the hymn
still hears an Adam singing on his own

his Eve-less garden, shamefaced that his bone
might call him out, might know his claim of prim
and walled and centred on that not yet grim
All-Knowing Face is struggle with his own
reflection, so, dear boy, you'll have a crone
to mourn you amidst her green world's vim.

I was a woman once the poet saw
mumbling the edges of the world a-flaw,
so bishop never set it perfect. Flesh,
the lovely beast, must sin to know. Awe
's at once! After, no word has it fresh.
No will speaks trust, nor lies a throat seen blush.

No will-struck tryst but pleads a throat seen blush
will help its credence change another will,
the both to serve a great, imploring Will
that raises same the child from time's onrush,
and only after, when the hunger's flush
with satisfactions, time itself seems still,
showing garden thru the world's seams, no ill
or fear or doubt, none of life's ambush,

for dead don't care they've lived. The dead don't fear.
The dead have nothing that they want to hear.
That blossom flourish, bee still husband, wind
still stride the grasses, Jane be victim's peer,
the dead let go, as words entiding mind
wherein the you and I continue twinned.

Here, in each you, the I continues twined,
that oldest paradox each side has guessed
alone within a skull. You are the rest
of me, the held heft gardening this mind.
Bone vault what cell, how well the sea will grind
its evidence away, transforming crest
to trough and founding infinite, if stressed
singular, tellings, combed, carded, combined.

Say Helen never died. Say Egypt claimed
some little of her true, and unashamed
a myth should put down roots, should never flee
purged by forgetting wastes to sow unnamed
some chance-sprouted future, by this sea,
'You pressed the seal in life,' she'll say of me.

Jane's Last Sea Song

A dream of whale decides me free
of drudging blood-thick, seed-spilled land.
Sea grants whale kinder gravity
than earth uprightly plumbs my stand,
and washes thin-gleaned charity
the grudging master will pretend.

One gasp of whale so dared and deep
is larger breath than I can share
for plunging past my shallow sleep
down its darkly smallest air,
but grasp a safeness I may keep
among the fortunes foundling there.

Oh, that the just law were the whale's
that chooses sound the chasm, man,
at whose blank bottom lie those tales
midwifed my hope as I began,
the sea were where no justice fails
to dream what I no longer can.

ACKNOWLEDGMENTS

My thanks to the Nova Scotia Department of Tourism and Culture for a writing grant that aided in the creation of this work,

and, of course, to M.J. Edwards, whose insightful declamations helped make clear the music, and whatever else endures.

ABOUT THE AUTHOR

M.J. EDWARDS

Wayne Clifford is the author of seven books of poetry. His most recent collections are *The Book of Were, On Abducting the 'Cello*, and *The Exile's Papers, Part One: The Duplicity of Autobiography* all published by The Porcupine's Quill. Clifford has published poems in an incredibly broad range of journals – from *Canadian Forum* to avant-garde magazines like bill bissett's *Blewointment*, bpNichol's *ganglia*, and Sheila Watson's *White Pelican*. He lives on Grand Manan where the benign seclusion of obscurity is conducive to sonneteering.